To
Chris an

D1826435

A SELECTION OF CREEPY SHORT STORIES

By Elisa J Wilkinson

Best wishes,.

Elisa Wilkinson

Every story in my book holds an element of truth.

Published by New Generation Publishing in 2023

First Edition

Paperback ISBN: 978-1-80369-656-0
eBook ISBN: 978-1-80369-657-7

www.newgeneration-publishing.com

New Generation Publishing

DEDICATION

I dedicate this book to my daughter Lesley Anne, who after the age of thirteen managed to overcome her fears of psychic phenomena. After experiencing the spirit figure of a man in the road Lesley overcame her fear of the paranormal. She now joins me with my psychic investigations and public interviews.

Contents

THE RING

"Oh my goodness, I can`t believe it, it`s snowing" Mary groaned when peeping out from behind the lace curtains hanging at her window,

"It`s the middle of May, we shouldn`t be having snow at this time of the year".

"Well it is cold enough" her husband, Tom, grumbled coming to her side and watching as the thick snowflakes settled on the window sill of their cottage.

"I think you two ought to be making tracks home before it gets worse," he added in a worried tone,

"On the other hand, you could stay the night and go back tomorrow".

"I don`t think so dad, but thanks all the same. It could be worse in the morning and you know what the weather gets like out here at Greenhough. It`s also a steep hill down to Pateley."

"Hm," David`s father nodded, "the hills are pretty steep out here, and all the way back to Harrogate come to think of it.

"Aye lad your right. You`d better get moving if you want to get home safely"

"Turn the heating up will you Mary, we want the bedroom warm don`t we?" Tom muttered as he picked up his pipe and newspaper, then settled himself in the cosy armchair near the fire.

Mary threw Helen her daughter in law a disparaging, why glance, then shrugged and went down the hall to turn up the heating.

"Dad`s right, we should be leaving David said after he peered through the window and noticed that the trees surrounding the cottage were beginning to bend in the strong breeze and that the snow on the open land was settling around his parents` home at Greenhough North Yorkshire. "The snowfall looks pretty heavy to me," he said, "and we have over an hour`s drive to get home, plus there`s a strong wind getting up,"

After making their farewells, David and Helen began their long hazardous trek home.

The wind was rising fast in the open country side and David had to struggle to keep his vehicle under control, when each gust of wind caught him sideways almost pushing the four wheel drive off the road.

"Bloody hell, it`s worse than I expected. Maybe dad was right, we should have stayed over" David grumbled. Then took his foot off the accelerator and braked when he spotted the dark figure of a woman moving furtively about the road up ahead.

"What on earth is she doing?" Helen whispered, staring through the blanket of snow, as she tried to make out the blurry figure. "It`s definitely a woman", David commented softly, "But what the hell is she doing wandering about the road in this weather, and at this time of night?" "My goodness" Helen stated as they drew closer.

"Do you think that was her car that we saw further back up the road?, maybe it has broken down.

"Never mind the car, look at her coat," David gestured towards the woman`s clothing.

"The sleeves are torn and covered with sludge, and those shoes, she should be wearing boots in this weather"

"But it might not have been so bad when she left home, and she`s not wearing a hat".

Helen remarked when seeing the woman`s long blonde hair blowing in every direction.

"David, she must have something wrong with her, we`ve got to stop and help her". "I know that," he muttered, pulling up alongside the bedraggled woman.

Helen felt a cold chill hit her when she wound down the car window.

"Can we give you a lift?" Helen called loudly to make herself heard above the roaring wind.

For a moment the woman stopped what she was doing, straightened up, and gave them a broad smile.

"She`s beautiful,"` Helen whispered to David, when seeing the woman`s violet blue eyes and perfectly formed features. She did however notice that under her long blonde hair she was wearing a pair of emerald and gold earrings that were encrusted with diamonds. They appeared to be exclusive and extremely expensive.

"It`s alright thank you" she replied, straightening her gloves.

"It won`t be too long before I find it, but thank you all the same",

She then carried on scrambling about the road side as if searching for something.

David shook his head in disbelief.

"There`s nothing we can do, we can`t force her to get into the car if we did, she might contact the police, then we`d be accused of kidnapping"

"But we can`t just leave her here, she will freeze to death in this weather" Helen argued.

"No Helen, think woman, think, if she has something wrong with her then she could accuse us of anything she wanted to. If that were to happen then we would really be in serious trouble. Not only that, but she could have escaped from a mental facility and might be dangerous".

"I didn`t think of that," Helen responded, as David pulled out his cell phone.

"Damn, there`s no reception," he cursed.

"We`ll stop at the first place we come across and ring the police from there they can go pick her up if that`s alright with you?"

"I agree," Helen sat nodding her head as she watched the woman, who appeared oblivious to the cold, reaching into the deep snow while scouring about the kerb edge.

"It`s the only thing we can do and the woman is definitely acting rather oddly".

It was the longest, most treacherous journey down to Pateley Bridge that David had ever made, and he breathed a sigh of relief when he saw the pub come into view.

"It's a bit late," he murmured to himself as he pulled onto the empty car park.

"But I don`t think the owner will mind when I explain the circumstances to him and ask if I can ring the police. You wait here in the car," he said, turning to Helen.

"It`s too cold for you out there".

Helen sat waiting patiently while David went to the door and knocked loudly until the publican opened the door and ushered him into the warmth of the building.

"What`s up lad, has tha got a problem?" Has tha broken down?" he asked in concern.

"No, it`s nothing like that" David replied, shaking his head he told him that it was an emergency and he needed to use the phone to call the police as he couldn't get any reception on his cell phone.

The publican then ushered him through to the bar to where the phone was situated, David thanked him and dialled the emergency services and was immediately put through to the police department, whereupon he told the officer what he and Helen had just witnessed. The officer listened patiently before telling David that what he had seen was the ghost of a woman, who was often seen on that particular stretch of road whenever it was snowing.

"What. You don`t mean?" he gasped The officer then went on to explain, that the woman had stopped her car when a call of nature had arisen. She had gone into the hedge bottom to relieve herself, but during the course of removing her gloves, she had pulled off her diamond engagement ring that her late mother had given her and it had dropped into the deep snow where she then couldn't find it. But upon hearing a car approaching, she had run out into the road to stop the driver to ask if he would help search for her missing ring.

But the snow had been falling so heavily that the driver did not see her until the last moment and his car had hit and killed her. Ever since that fateful night, she had been seen on that particular area of road whenever it was snowing, searching for the missing ring.

The officer told David not to worry about it and that he would send out a car immediately to ensure no one was in trouble. Then asked for his contact details and informed David that he would let him know if they needed to speak to him again. David was shaken by what he had heard , and after thanking the publican, he returned to Helen in the car and told her what the police officer had said.

For a few short moments they both sat in silence, before David started the car again and moved cautiously forward.

But as they passed through Summer Bridge and Burnt Yates, where the snow had settled, the drive was horrendous. It wasn't until they reached Killinghall that David managed to relax before finally reaching their home on the outskirts of Harrogate.

Once they were inside the house, he immediately rang his parents to tell them that they were safely home and what had happened. His father listened quietly to what David told him, then dropped the bombshell.

"I never told you, David, as your mother and I always felt it distressing whenever the subject arose in conversation……. but it was me who was driving the car that killed the young woman.

LITTLE MISS CHATTERBOX

"Jane, Jane, where are you?"

Jane could hear her husband, Bob, opening and closing the doors calling for her.

"I'm in here, the kitchen" she called out.

"Jane, I've found it, you will never believe it, it's perfect"

"What's perfect, what are you talking about," she asked in a puzzled tone when he burst into the room full of enthusiasm.

"I didn't expect you home until one o clock".

"Never mind that, come and sit down, I have something to tell you," his voice was filled with excitement as he pulled out a chair motioning for her to be seated.

"But the dinner,"

"Never mind that just now, I have something more important to tell you,

Jane gave a silent groan; she was used to him coming up with new, and what he called important, ideas.

"When me and Gordon went to price that job over on the coast road towards Mulgrove Castle, we passed a nice little area of Sandsend and stopped for a cup of tea. Afterwards, we decided to go for a walk to get a feel of the area, and that was when David got talking to one of the residents who told us about a derelict Dorma cottage that's not far from the sea. As luck would have it, he knew who the owner was and that she had been trying to get rid of it for ages. It wasn't locked so David took me to see it while he went to look at the job".

At that moment the phone rang,

"You get it" Jane told him, "It will most probably be for you"

Bob got up and lifted the receiver then slammed it down.

"Bloody sales people, you can never understand what they are garbling on about" he muttered angrily.

"Right, I was telling you about the cottage"

Jane nodded, at that moment all she could think about was preparing the food for dinner.

"The cottage roof is thatched, but the problem there is that the thatch is buggered and there are big holes in it, but the advantage is that it stands in its own grounds and has large gardens at both the back and front".

"Right now though it is overgrown with weeds, but I can soon cut them back and there is an added bonus" he said smiling smugly.

"The cottage doesn't have a preservation order on it so we could replace the thatched roof with tiles, that's only if you wanted to, and there`s a wild rose bush growing around the arched porch".

"But what is it like inside?, It will be damp if the roof has a hole in it, and is there any gas or electricity? Is it set on the main drains, which I doubt very much, with it being situated so far away from the town", she asked shaking her head in despair. "Well, there`s a bit of damp here and there, but what would you expect from a property that's been abandoned for the last fifteen or more years, especially when there`s a hole in the roof".

"Oh Robert" she chided, "There has to be a reason for it to have been left empty for so long", and shuddered at the thought of it having mice and rats nesting inside.

But nothing was going to deter Robert. "I don`t know, I didn't ask," he rambled on." Anyway, it has a long entrance hall that leads into a large kitchen` two decent sized sitting rooms` a smaller room that would be ideal for me to use as an office` three large bedrooms, one for us, one for our daughter Sarah, and a medium sized box room that could be turned into a spare bedroom. It would be ideal for Debbie when Valerie brings her to stay".

Debbie was Valerie`s only child, and the pair often stayed with them when Valerie`s husband was working abroad.

Before Jane had the chance to argue, the phone rang it was Gordon saying that he had found the last remaining relative of the latter owner who had died. It was a Mrs Becket, and she was willing to negotiate a price for the sale of the property, whereby he had arranged for them to go meet her and view the cottage the following weekend.

The following Saturday, Jane and Robert arrived at the home of the elderly owner Mrs Beckett. And after drinking endless cups of tea, she suggested that they drove out to the cottage to inspect it thoroughly before making their decision. She then informed them that the cottage was never kept locked so they wouldn't need a key.

This surprised Robert and Jane: although the cottage door had been left open when Robert and Graham sneaked in to take a look around, they still thought it a bit odd and voiced their concern at the thought of her leaving a cottage unlocked for such a long period of time, especially as it was filled with antique furniture and other items of value.

But Mrs Becket waved her hand at the idea of someone wanting to rob her and asked if they wanted another cup of tea. That they readily declined, telling her that Robert had another property to view before making up his mind about Rose Cottage.

Nevertheless, after they did finally manage to get away from Mrs Beckett and her endless gossip, and cups of tea, they got into the car and drove away.

As Robert drove along the narrow twisting country road, Jane was pleased to see that the school, the hospital, and the doctor`s surgery were situated close to the small village that they had driven through.

She was also pleased to find that the cottage was only one and a half miles away from the village, and was in a secluded spot in a glade of trees hidden away from prying eyes.

However, at the sight and smell of damp and decay, Jane could feel an aura of depression settling upon her shoulders. Robert loved it, and the scurrying mice, plus cobwebs did nothing to deter him as he checked out every conceivable space in each room. He did, however, groan when after going outside to check the outer exterior of the building, he found that the doors and windows were rotten and would need replacing. In fact, the whole place would need gutting to make it habitable and the roof needed to be replaced.

In the meantime, Jane had gone outside to look around the garden and was surprised when a little girl of around eight years old, the same age as her own daughter, crept through a gap in the hedge followed by a huge black Labrador dog.

"Are you coming to live here?" she asked brushing the leaves and dust from her clothing that looked rather old fashioned and dated. "My name is Emma, and this is Blackie. She introduced her dog who gave a friendly wag of his tail as he seated himself beside Emma, who stood fiddling with her long plaited hair. "Can I come and play here until you move in? Old Mrs Becket, who used to live here, didn't like us and she used to shout at me to go away".

"Of course you can. You can come whenever you like and you can play with my daughter Sarah. It will be nice for her to have someone her own age to play with. Do you have any special friends Emma"?

"I have Blackie, he is my best friend", Emma replied.

"I shall have to be going now, goodbye". She turned and scrambled through the hedge.

"What do you think to the place"? Robert asked when he came out of the house and into the garden.

"Who were you talking to"

Before she had the chance to reply to his questions, he asked, "Could you live here?"

"Well", she hesitated for a moment, and looked at her husband and immediately knew when seeing the eager expression on his face that she would never have heard the end of it if she turned the property down. It`s a bit of a mess, but you know it`s what I`ve always dreamed of" she replied.

"Then it is yours", he said, flinging his big strong arms about her and giving her a hug.

In a matter of weeks the cottage had been transformed into a beautiful home: the new roof and the rewiring had been a huge expense, and so had the oil central heating. Every room was redecorated: new windows and doors had replaced the rotted old ones, and in the two large bedrooms, Robert had fitted on-suit bathrooms: and downstairs, was a brand new modern kitchen. The adjoining outbuilding had been turned into a toilet and utility room: new carpets were laid, and the antique furnishings left behind that they purchased from Mrs Backet blended in perfectly with the style of the old cottage.

As the weeks passed, both Jane and Robert gradually fell into the routine of the tiny village, they were made welcome by being invited to garden parties, home cooking events and knitting for the church bazaar. They even christened Emma, Little Miss Chatterbox as she never stopped talking.

A problem arose one day however, while Jane was alone in the kitchen, the peace and quiet was unexpectedly interrupted when she heard the sound of a child`s laughter coming from the playroom.

`Whoever can it be? she wondered`, It can`t be Sarah she`s at school, Jane listened for a few moments longer before going to investigate but when opening the door and glancing about the playroom, she found that it was empty. Then became alarmed when the smell of burning filled her nostrils.

"Oh my goodness the dinner", Jane gasped thinking that one of the pans had boiled over and dashed back into the kitchen. She was relieved to find that the pans were bubbling normally and nothing was spoilt.

That evening, when Robert arrived home from work, Jane told him about hearing the laughter, but he said it was nothing to worry about, and that it could have been a fox, or some other creature. There were always strange sounds coming from animals roaming about the open land and he left it at that. Nevertheless Jane was not convinced by what Robert was saying, and was thankful that Sarah was staying the night at the home of one of her new school friends. But that evening as they were sat quietly in the lounge they were they both startled when unexpectedly hearing the sound of a child's laughter ringing throughout every room of the cottage.

"What the devil" Robert dropped the book he was reading and sprang to his feet endeavouring to hear which room the noise was coming from.

"It's coming from the playroom", Jane whispered putting down the embroidery she was doing and grabbed hold of Robert's arm.

"I told you that I had heard it earlier".

Without further hesitation they raced down the hall to the playroom where to their surprise the laughter stopped immediately that they opened the door.

They were, however, shocked to find that the toys that had been neatly packed away, were strewn all over the floor and the rocking horse was swaying backwards and forwards as if someone was riding it.

"What the hell's going on?" Robert gasped. "I thought you said Sarah was staying with her friend tonight"

"She is", Jane stammered, equally perplexed,

"Come on I'll help to pick up the toys and pack them away" he said before returning to the lounge. The following day, Robert was concerned about leaving Jane alone in the cottage while he left to discuss a new business contract he had been offered.

But she told him not to worry she would be all right and that she was going to do some gardening.

As soon as he was gone Jane went out into the garden to trim the roses, but as soon as she had picked up the sectators, Emma squeezed through the hedge quickly followed by Blackie.

"Oh I'm pleased you're here" Jane said petting the dog.

"Would you help me to pick some strawberries for lunch, then we can have strawberries and cream".

Little Emma`s face lit up, and within minutes, she had raced into the cottage and returned with a bowl for the fruit.

"Would you stay and look after the house while I pop into the village to pick up something I forgot earlier?. There`s orange juice in the fridge if you want it, just help yourself".

"Thank you" Emma replied, giving a light courtesy, then stuffed her mouth full of the delicious berries. Jane got into her car, drove to the village and bought what she needed from the grocery store then called in to the butcher.

"Good morning Mrs Johnson I`ve got the nice joint of beef that you ordered and the sausage" "Oh, could I have a few bones for the dog please?" she asked.

"So, you've got yourself a pet have you?" Mr Benson said, with a smile, as he parcelled everything together.

"No, not really. A little girl, Emma, has taken a shine to visiting me and the dog belongs to her, they are absolutely devoted to one another, and she never stops talking, Robert and I have named her Little Miss chatterbox".

Jane noticed that Mr Benson was looking at her with an odd expression on his face. "You say her name is Emma?"

Jane nodded.

"Is she polite and well dressed, and is the dog a big black Labrador?".

"Why, yes", Jane replied, "how did you know" "My God, heaven protect you," he said in a worried tone.

A sudden chill and the sense of fear drifted through Jane.

"What is it? What`s wrong?" she stammered when feeling a sense of alarm pass through her?

"That cottage where you live Mrs Johnson," he stammered hardly knowing where to begin. "Go on" she urged, "What about the cottage?"

There was a fire there one night, many, many, years ago. Nobody knew how it started but by the time the fire brigade got there it was too late. The place was practically gutted and everyone in there died. I was just a lad when it happened but I`ll never forget that blaze it was horrible. The firemen did all they could to save the family but when they managed to get inside they found the couple laid as if they were asleep in bed. They were dead. The firemen said that the smoke and fumes must have choked them. They found their eight year old daughter laying on the floor with her arms around her dog as if she was trying to protect the animal: both had suffocated".

"The little girl's name was Emma, and her dog was called Blackie".

Jane felt her stomach churn at what he told her.

"Well thank you Mr Benson, but maybe you are mistaken, Emma is waiting for me back at the cottage, where she is picking strawberries so that she can have them with me when I return."

Mr Benson stared after her, shaking his head, as she left the shop, got into her car, and drove away. She didn't see the look of concern on his face as he lifted the phone.

Robert had arrived home by the time Jane had returned from her shopping spree Emma had washed and prepared the strawberry's that she had placed in a dish, and had also got a jug ready for the cream.

"I've brought some bones for Blackie" Jane said, placing the bag on the table, "it's only right that he should join in the party".

Emma squealed with delight,

"Can we can eat outside, and watch Blackie eat his bones?"

"Of course we can" Jane replied.

"Come on Blackie", Emma disappeared outside where they could hear her talking and singing to the dog.

Jaye and Robert followed with the food, Emma gave the bones to Blackie, while they sat themselves down to enjoy the fresh strawberries and cream. At the same time Blackie buried two of the bones, then settled down and lay gnawing at the last one.

Then after a while Blackie began nuzzling Emma's hand.

"I'm sorry but we shall have to be going" Emma informed them.

"Thank you for the tea, and Blackie says thank you for his bones, whereby the dog gave a deep throaty woof as Emma gave Jane and Robert a shy kiss on the cheek, then scrambled through the hedge after him.

"She's an affectionate little thing" said Robert, "and she's certainly taken a liking to you" "Yes she seems to have," Jane replied. The following day Jane drove into the village and upon seeing Mr Benson, the butcher, she called out to him,

"I just want to tell you that Emma had tea with us and Blackie enjoyed one of his bones: the rest are buried in the flower beds". She couldn't exactly tell what he said as he walked away, but it sounded like, May God protect you both`

That evening after dinner and when Sarah was fast asleep in her own room, they were about to retire for the night when they suddenly caught the waft of smoke.

"Oh my God" Jane cried in alarm.

It's coming from the playroom and I can hear someone in there"

Robert and Jane leapt to their feet and dashed along the hallway to where Robert cautiously opened the playroom door.

What the hell?" Robert gasped, then turned to Jane.

"Stay back" he ordered abruptly when seeing that the room was filled with clouds of drifting smoke. And He threw her a warning glance. Then suddenly they heard a child's cries of delight and laughter emanating from the centre of the smoke filled room making their blood run cold.

Within seconds however the smoke began to clear, leaving a full vision of Emma, who was shrieking with joy, as she sat with her arms filled with toys sitting astride the wooden rocking horse, while Blackie was chasing a ball across the floor.

Jane was shocked beyond belief and put her hand to her mouth to stop herself from crying out. "I can't believe what I am seeing" she whispered, while Robert stood staring speechless at the sight of Emma and Blackie.

As if becoming aware of the couple watching, Blackie stopped chasing the ball and gave a gruff welcoming bark and ran to greet them, while Emma climbed down from the rocking horse and hurried forward. Then with tears in her beautiful blue eyes she looked up at Jane and Robert.

"I'm sorry if I have upset you but I just wanted to play with the toys for the last time, I never had any toys like these and it was such fun for the little time I had left".

Jane and Robert threw one another a puzzled glance

"I don't understand, Emma", Robert said. "You know you can come and play anytime you like?".

Emma took a step forward and reached out to take hold of their hands

"I love you both, really I do, and so does Blackie"

The dog wagged his tail and licked Robert's hand, then he moved back to Emma. "Goodbye Jane, Goodbye Robert thank you for sharing everything with us it has been so nice. Now we can go home".

Within minutes Emma and Blackie slowly faded away. "Oh no; no;" Jayne sobbed. "Emma, Blackie come back, please, where are you?"

Although he was shaken by the uncanny events, Bob took hold of Jane who was sopping uncontrollably. "Come on love, we've made them both happy by making them welcome in our home. Now, let's have a cup of tea and go to bed"

Although Robert was feeling as devastated as Jane, he tried not to show it, he was going to miss the noisy mischievous pair as much as his wife. She was however, so distressed at the thought of losing Emma and Blackie, who had become part of the family, had to take a sleeping pill to get her through the night. Robert sat in his chair, drinking tea and smoking his pipe deep in thought.

The following day was utter chaos: everyone from the village had heard the devastating news and had hurried to the cottage.

"We were too late" the fireman Charlie Simpson, told Frank Hemsworth the local storekeeper. "They were a lovely couple and so was their little girl" Mr Benson, the butcher, added tearfully.

"They must have been overcome by the fumes, I heard they never tried to escape" one local resident whispered to another.

"It`s strange the same thing this happening to them as it did to that other family; you know them with the little girl and her dog? That cottage was always strange, that's why the old lady wouldn't live there, and none of the locals would touch it either".

"I remember, everybody round here saying it was haunted.

HENRY

The long silky tresses of her soft auburn hair slid effortlessly through his fingers as he cupped her elfin face in his hands and gazed into her pale blue eyes. "I love you Melissa", he said, tenderly wiping a tear from her cheek with a kiss,

"I'm sorry darling; that I have to leave you at a time like this, but I cannot avoid this business trip. You above all should understand how much it means to me and the company that I attend the meeting".

Melissa didn't answer, without altering her gaze, she just sat staring stoically in front of her.

"I will ring you as soon as I arrive in Paris," he said with a sigh, rising from her bedside, then walked over to the dressing table mirror on the pretext of straightening his tie. He watched for her reaction in the glass, but there was none.

"How ironic life is," he pondered in silent sadness, as he gazed at her beautiful face reflecting in the mirror. Over confidence and complacency had brought about his downfall, he had never expected Melissa to find out about Penny, yet she had, and it had devastated her.

As for himself, in those two days of being alone with Penny he had suddenly realised what a degenerative creature he had become.

He now wanted to make amends and start over again with his wife, proclaiming emphatically how much he loved her, and that he had never slept with Penny which was undeniably true.

It was too late however, for in the days he was gone, Melissa had hired a private detective who had been watching, photographing and recording every move he had made. Then, when he had returned home, there was an unexpected shock awaiting him when Melissa told him that she had filed for divorce.

After hours of emotional bickering and tears, Melissa had made it quite clear that there would be no chance of a reconciliation. He had hurt and embarrassed her for the last time, she could no longer live with his philandering ways therefore he must leave.

Heartbroken, Henry forced his mind back to the present. He hesitated for a few moments longer, savouring every second of her beautiful image reflecting in the mirror, before turning towards her.

"I'll be going now", his voice cracked with emotion "If by any chance you change" he stopped what he was saying in midsentence, when realising from the strained look on her face he should say no more.

Filled with despondency and remorse, he placed his last item of value into his overnight bag and left the bedroom. Then he cringed and almost cried out when after closing the door behind himself, he heard the sound of China dishes shattering, when the breakfast tray he had brought up for his wife tumbled to the floor breaking everything in its wake.

Half blinded by tears, Henry stumbled down the wide sweeping staircase, where in a moment of anger, he kicked the slippers from his feet sending them pivoting across the marbled entrance hall floor.

Unable to control his emotions any longer Henry finally broke down and sobbed with uncontrollable frustration at the futility of the situation, knowing that it was his own stupid fault that had brought him to this. Then, after a time when the tears had begun to slow, Henry reached into the hall cupboard for his overcoat and trilby hat, knowing full well that he would be doing this for the last time in his wife's ancestral home. He flopped onto the window seat to pull on his brown brogue shoes.

The moment Henry leant back against the cold grey mullioned stone window of the mansion, he became acutely aware of what he had lost and was leaving behind. Yet it did offer him some consolation to be able to accept and adapt to the changes that were forthcoming.

Gradually, positive ideas began to form in his legal constructive mind, when after lacing up his shoes and getting to his feet, he looked about his home.

"This house and its land should fetch a tidy sum especially to a builder: two of the cars can be sold: so should the villas in France and Italy, that's if she agrees. What the hell, it was what I earned that paid to keep everything going, so, why should she end up living in style?. Bugger it, I'll get rid of as much as I can and that should give me some spare cash. Even Melissa doesn't know how many assets I've secreted away over the years into offshore bank accounts. "Dam", he cursed glancing at his watch.

His flight didn't leave until 5-30pm. "Not to worry", he told himself. He would go straight to the hotel where he would be meeting his colleagues who would be assembling there for a briefing before taking the flight to the lawyers' conference in Paris.

Henry hesitated for a few moments longer to take a last look at the home he was about to relinquish. Then after opening the front door, he picked up his luggage and marched confidently to the Bentley where he packed everything into the boot of the car, except for the leather bag which he placed on the seat beside himself and drove steadily away, thinking "This is another phase of my life that is over, now is the time for some radical changes."

Oscar was surprised to see Henry entering the VIP lounge of the hotel so early and gestured for him to join him, where within minutes they were enjoying a few drinks together.

Oscar had noticed however, the pale drawn look on Henry's face but had declined to comment.

Nevertheless, he was dumbfounded when Henry dropped his bombshell by revealing that he was considering leaving the legal profession.

"But you can't," Oscar stammered in amazement.

"You're one of the top leading barristers in the country, and Melissa, what does she have to say about this, surely she?"

Henry cut him off before he could finish what he was saying.

"Stuff Melissa and everybody else!" Henry shouted, as all heads turned to stare at them.

"They can all go to hell".

Oscar found himself speechless. He was so overcome by Henry's emotional outburst, that he could only watch in shock as Henry snatched up the bag beside him and slammed out of the dining room.

Henry was so enraged by Oscar's questions, that he never bothered to retrieve his hat and coat from the waiter standing by the door. He just wanted to get away from all of the gawping faces surrounding him. Oblivious to the strange looks cast in his direction, Henry pushed his way through the crowded hotel to the foyer, where the doorman had noticed the thunderous expression on the approaching man's face.

He immediately leapt to attention when recognising him and saluted as he pulled the door open for the irate guest to depart, while at the same time signalling to the valet to bring Henry's car to the door.

Henry didn't wait though. Once outside, he suddenly felt a whole lot better when the crisp winter's air circulated around him. Cooling his temper and allowing him to think in a more positive frame of mind. Clutching the bag closely to his chest, Henry made his way over to the Harrogate Arms, where he cut through the pinewoods, then out towards Birk Crag, determined not to stop until he had reached his destination on the desolate moors.

Then dropping to his knees and waiting only long enough for him to recover his breath, Henry removed a digging trowel from his bag and began scraping away at the hard, frozen soil at the base of the huge boulder and didn't stop until he had completed a deep circular hole.

Shattered, he leant back against the boulder recalling the last few days, wishing that he could turn back the clock to March 13th. Poor Melissa, he had had to force her to keep silent about his last disastrous fling as she had been threatening to disclose all of the latest sordid details in their divorce proceedings. How was he to know that Penny, the woman he had picked up in a nightclub, was a sex change bisexual?. Heaven forbid, it would have ruined him if that had got out: he couldn't let her broadcast that.

One thing he knew for certain was, that Penny would never tell: she had been taken care of when he had thrown the freak into the Strid at Bolton Abbey, the whirlpool had sucked her body straight down to where no one would ever find the loathsome creature. That part of the river was supposed to be bottomless, no bodies had ever been recovered from there.

Furthermore, if it hadn't been for that meddlesome detective Melissa had hired, he would have been in the clear, and they would still be together.

"Curse and damn him" he had to die he had witnessed everything the women, the hotels, the photographs he had taken as evidence.

The offer of a few thousand pounds to keep quiet about the whole mess had been enough to tempt the greedy swine to a meeting up at the Cow and Calf at Ilkley Moor. Henry had filled him full of Whiskey before helping him over the steep edge of the rock face. The coroner and police had agreed that he must have wondered over in a drunken stupor, he was known to enjoy a drink or more, whereby Henry was in the clear.

Henry chuckled to himself as he clambered to his feet and stretched. Then after taking a short walk around the boulder to get his circulation working properly, he returned and knelt in front of the hole he had prepared earlier. After opening and reaching into his bag, Henry brought out and unwrapped the precious package and brought its contents close to his face.

Dried congealed blood and trailing tendrils of sinew and vein hung down from the dismembered head of his once beautiful wife, Melissa. Her glazed blood filled eyes stared unblinking back at him from her black sunken eye sockets, in the remains of her discoloured face. In his bizarre realms of fantasy, she remained to him not only the exquisite, intellectual woman who had stood beside him as a Queen's Councillor in the supreme High Court, but as a passionate desirable woman. In his befuddled mind she was gazing back at him through clear blue eyes, filled with love and adoration, and whose sensuous mouth awaited the passionate kiss as he pressed his lips against hers.

Then with a tearful farewell, he gently lowered the nauseating residue of her remains into the hole that he had created and covered it with soil. He rose to his feet and without a backward glance, turned and walked away.

Cut that's perfect"; the film director's voice echoed around the silent studio, "print it" And he walked over to Henry to congratulate him.

"You carried out the last scene perfectly, just as if you had really done it," he said jovially, patting Henry on the back.

"There's a bonus in this for you. You were terrific: you're not only a bloody good actor, but my, God, a dammed brilliant writer as well. You really had me believing you had actually done it".

"Please, no more" Henry said holding up his hands in false submission.

"I can't take it," he began to laugh.

"Got to give credit where credits due," the director called, as his new found genius turned and walked away. The director never saw Henry's secretive smile as he returned to his dressing room, nor did he hear him murmur.

"A good actor? Huh, that is something you will never know, the legal profession is full of actors".

Only one person did not come forward to congratulate Henry after watching his outstanding performance, and that was Chief Inspector Jay,

He knew about Henry`s sordid past and had his own role to play now.

THE SCHOOL BOY

Gary and Linda Byron were still in their nightclothes, and had just finished eating breakfast when they heard the doorbell ring.

"Bloody Hell" Gary groaned, it`s only just gone seven, who the Dickins can be ringing the doorbell this early." He grumbled stifling a yawn.

"I`ll go," Linda muttered sliding from her seat and pulling her dressing gown tightly around herself. She slid her feet into her slippers then shuffled across the kitchen floor, and into the hallway to open the door. Where she was surprised to see a cheerful, well dressed young man standing at the door.

"Hello, I`m Brian Roberts" he said, holding out his hand as he introduced himself.

"I rang earlier about the Classic car that you have advertised for sale in the local paper".

"Oh yes, won`t you come in? I`ll tell my husband you`re here but we didn't expect you so early" she said, ushering him into the living room where he sat waiting for Gary.

In the meantime, Gary who had overheard Brian speaking to Linda, had rushed into the bathroom, rinsed his face with cold water to wake himself up, quickly shaved and dressed, then combed his hair before going into the sitting room to meet Brian.

"This is a surprise," he said shaking Brian`s hand.

"We only put the advertisement in the paper a couple of days ago, we didn't know that it had gone in until you rang last night." Gary stifled another yawn.

Gary and Linda had been awoken by the phone ringing at ten pm the previous night with Brian enquiring about the car. Ever since his retirement almost a year ago Gary had become accustomed to sleeping in and not having to worry about getting up early to catch the commuter train into work.

Nevertheless, He told Brian that he was surprised that the add had been answered so quickly.

"Yes, but a classic Mercedes convertible car! And as you stated in the advertisement, in immaculate condition with such low mileage. Well," Brian gestured with his hands. "At the price you are asking, it is something that you don't come across very often, is it?".

Before Gary could reply his wife Linda, asked Brian, if he would like a cup of tea or coffee.

"Sorry, but I must decline your kind offer as I have a dentist appointment in an hour`s time and I don`t want to be late." Brian pointed to his watch and turned to Gary.

"If it`s not too inconvenient for you, could I see the car now please?"

The moment Brian asked to see the car, he became aware that someone was watching them. And felt an unanticipated sense of unease sweep through him, when a boy aged about ten years old, short and thin, dressed in a pale grey school uniform with a green insignia on the top pocket of his jacket, and a peaked grey cap tilted sideways on his head, peeped at him from the doorway beneath the stairs.

Ignoring the child, Brian turned and followed Gary, who directed him to a door leading along the hallway then through another door that took them directly into the garage.

"I got the idea of having the garage built adjoining the house after working and living in America a number of years ago. It helps to keep us dry when we have our unstable British weather," he added with a grin.

"It`s a good idea Brian replied, as he followed Gary into the garage, "I might do the same myself; that's if I can get planning permission. You know what bastards the planners can be?.

Brian`s face reddened when he realised that Linda was standing behind them. "Sorry" he murmured turning to Linda. "I do apologise for my terminology of language"

"That's alright, most people feel the same way as you do about the local authorities, so you don`t need to apologise,"

Gary walked over to the car that was encased in sheets and carefully removed them.

"Oh my god, it is beautiful," Brian uttered, thoroughly enthralled by the vehicles immaculate condition.

"Theres no scratches on the paintwork, the chrome is perfect, there`s no cracks in the leather upholstery the floor mats are in good condition".

"Can I lift the mats to check underneath?" he asked hesitantly.

"Of course, take a good look at everything, there is a soft top beneath the hard top if you would care to see it, but I can assure you there are no water stains on it, we never took the car out in bad weather with the soft top covering it, we always used the hard one."

"I will show you," Gary unscrewed the hard top then showed Brian how to pull up the soft cover.

"Oh my God, it is so beautiful, Can I sit in it?" he asked in a shaky voice.

"You can take her for a run if you want," Gary said, unlocking the door and indicating for Brian to get into the driver`s seat. Instead, Brian reached inside and lovingly caressed the cream leather upholstery.

"It`s automatic, and convertible" he crooned in awe of the vehicles splendid condition.

"And the mileage is pretty decent for a car this age, and it`s so clean. There`s not a scratch or a mark on it, it looks almost brand new,"

"As I said, you can take her for a run if you like," Gary said with a smile.

"It would be preferable if you drove it out of the garage," Brian added hesitantly, as he once again noticed the boy in his grey school uniform and cap with its green insignia on the badge peeping round the door.

"Are you alright?" Gary asked when seeing the strange look on Brian`s face.

"Yes, er, yes," he nodded.

"Right then, let`s go" Gary climbed into the driver`s seat while Brian seated himself beside him Gary then switched on the engine that kicked in at the first turn. The deep rumbling throb of the car`s powerful engine sent ripples of excitement racing through Brian`s body as Gary carefully reversed out of the garage and out onto the road. Then, with a purring but thunderous roar, he accelerated away towards the highway.

"It is so smooth" Brian commented, "I`ve got to have it"

"I`ve always wanted a classic convertible, but this, it`s beyond belief Brian`s voice shook as he spoke.

However just as they drove into the garage they noticed Linda was speaking to someone on the phone attached to the garage wall. "I think you had better speak to my husband," she said, "we have a gentleman here who is already viewing the car"

Linda glanced over to Gary and Brian who had their heads under the bonnet.

"Gary can you take the phone?" she called placing her hand over the receiver.

There is a man offering several hundred pounds more than the asking price".

"What?" he gasped, "Just a minute" he said taking the phone from her shaking hand.

"Hello?, no it isn't sold yet but I have someone here who is very interested. Yes, yes, alright I`ll hold onto it until you`ve seen it".

Gary handed the phone back to Marjorie and returned to where Brian was standing by the car.

"I overheard what you were saying" Brian told Gary, and I am prepared to offer you the same amount of money as the other person offered."

"Well I told the man I would give him half an hour to get here before making a decision".

"Mr Byron, I want that car, it`s first come first served isn't it?"

27

Before he could say anymore Gary`s phone rang again. "Yes it`s still here. A gentleman is already here viewing the car, Yes it is a classic and in perfect running order, you will be here in fifteen minutes?. I have to tell you though, that I have been offered a larger amount than what I was asking for. Yes we will see you in a short while."

Brian wiped the sweat from his brow; he wanted the car, but the strain of other people offering more money and constant staring from the boy was making him even more nervous. He wished the child would go away but he didn't, instead he stood watching every move that Brian made.

Brian didn`t dare say anything about the child in case he jeopardised the deal regarding the car. Then felt his heart lurch with a sickening thud when a Rolls Royce car pulled up outside of the property followed by an immaculate classic Volkswagen car.

Both drivers got out of their vehicles and ignoring Brian, walked towards Gary.

"Is this the vehicle you have for sale?" the Rolls driver asked, flicking cigar ash onto the clean garage floor. He made his way slowly around the car and began inspecting its inner and outer exterior.

"Yes it is, and please do not drop any of that cigar ash onto the cars upholstery," Gary expressed, clearly annoyed by the man`s overbearing attitude. He then informed both men that he had already accepted a price for the car while he had been awaiting their arrival.

"But I offered you extra money for it;" the man shouted into Gary`s face. "Alright then, I`ll make it an extra one fifty," he blustered, "but I won`t go any higher"

"But I`ve already offered that," Brian added in frustration. He became even more annoyed when he heard the boy giggling from behind the door as all three bartered for the car.

"Make that fifty quid extra without the trial run," the Volkswagen driver offered. "But, but, bloody hell," Brian spluttered angrily, I thought…….."

"It's alright, it's yours" Gary interrupted turning to face an irate Brian.

"Come inside where we can draw up the vehicle exchange papers."

The two men couldn't believe it when Gary ushered them out of the garage and closed the door behind them. Neither of them noticed the boy; they had been too intent on getting their hands on the car at a bargain price.

Once inside the house Brian calmed down and thanked him, and asked why he had accepted his lower offer.

Gary then told him that he appeared to genuinely want the car for himself, and had a gut feeling that the other two men were dealers.

"I think you're right," Brian added, "but can I ask you something?".

"Go ahead"

"Does your grandson always stare at people like that?. He scares the hell out of me.

He's been watching and following us everywhere I didn't realise it at first but he managed to squeeze into the rear seat of the car when we took it for a test drive.

"He's alright, he's harmless" Gary responded with a smile. "He has a habit of watching and following people when they come to visit".

"Oh, Brian said, nodding as they completed the transaction ."It's been a pleasure doing business with you" Gary said, handing the car keys over to Brian and shaking his hand. Brian slid the documents into his jacket pocket and went over to the door.

"I'll see you to the car", Gary escorted Brian out to the garage and watched as he climbed into the car then carefully drove away.

But when Brian exited the drive, Gary had watched with a heavy heart, yet also with a sense of relief as the ghostly figure of the boy waved goodbye to him through the car's rear window.

Gary hadn't dared to tell Brian that he had been unable to drive the car in comfort after the distressing accident.

On the day of the accident, Gary had been aware that some of the school children ran out into the road when school was over. Therefore he had been driving very carefully when a young boy had suddenly emerged from behind a parked car. The boy however, had run into the side of Gary`s car, and the impact had pushed him over to the kerb edge where he had fallen and fractured his skull. He had later died from his injury.

The judge and jury had declared a verdict of misadventure and Gary was cleared of all blame.

Gary and Linda never saw the boy in their home again after the car was sold.

THE CONTESSA

"Oh boy, what a holiday," said Sandra as they boarded the plane for home.

"Well I don`t want another holiday like that," Janet moaned. "I feel as if every bone in my body is either bruised or broken" she remarked with a sour face, "and I`ve sprained my ankle."

She looked sorrowfully down at her bandaged limb.

"I hope I can still walk straight after this comes off"

Sandra gave her a nudge propelling her to her seat.

"Shut up you, miserable sod, think yourself lucky it wasn't worse, or as bad as Peter`s Injuries."

Peter however, wasn't going to join in with the girls` banter, he had enough problems of his own. He had ended up with his left leg and wrist encased in plaster.

"I will say this much for the holiday, I`ve never had so much rest," he grumbled hobbling, towards his seat, and dropped into it with a thud. "And I don`t want any of you telling them back home how I did this".

"It`s alright, Peter, your secret is safe with us; we`ll let them think that you did it on the ski slope."

That`s right," Bob added with a grin.

"We won`t tell the gang back at college that you were pissed and fell down the stairs."

His comments were met with howls of laughter while Peter grimaced and shrank back Into his seat.

The plane hadn't been airborne for long when a tremulous shudder shook the entire aircraft and the warning light came on overhead telling them to fasten their seat belts and to remain in their seats.

"What the hell could have caused that?" David remarked, glancing around at the passengers` frightened faces.

"I've no idea, most likely an air pocket," Bob replied casually.

"The hostess is coming our way so ask her."

When reaching Bob and David, Bob stopped her and asked if there was a problem. with the aircraft.

Smiling she told them not to worry and that everything was under control, it's just that they were flying through a storm and the wind was buffeting the plane a little.

"Well I've made this flight many times, but I've never experienced anything like this before," Bob remarked in a sardonic tone. He was totally unconvinced by what the stewardess had said as the stewardess went to speak to the other passengers who were also asking questions and feeling uneasy about the situation.

However the tension quickly grew amongst the passengers, when a violent flash of lightening hit the side of the plane sending it spinning helplessly off course in the storm filled sky. The roar of thunder could be clearly heard above the screams of terror, as the passengers who had been moving along the aisle were flung about the cabin and bombarded by the baggage. When the luggage locker doors flew open, scattering bags and parcels in all directions.

"Would everyone please be seated and fasten your seat belts," a voice suddenly boomed over the Intercom as the warning sign flickered on overhead. "We are experiencing a little turbulence"

"A little; You must be bloody joking" Bobs snarled derisively as he fastened his seat belt with trembling hands.

A sudden, violent shudder shook the body of the aircraft, followed by the engine's spluttering before becoming silent.

"Oh God" someone screamed. "We're going to crash"

Screams of extreme fear filled the aircraft when it suddenly began spiralling downwards towards the ground. Then to everyone's relief, it levelled out slightly.

"I think we're going to have to ditch her. Tell the passengers to be ready and take the necessary precaution" the captain informed the stewardess.

The hostesses face was ashen when she returned to the cabin and faced the passengers.

"Ladies and gentlemen, as you are now aware, we are having problems with the aircraft. The captain is preparing to make an emergency landing so if you would all take the crash positions then you will stand a good chance of survival".

"I told you we were going to crash!" an hysterical woman screamed.

"We`re all going to die"

"Shut up you silly cow, and do as the woman said," a male voice roared. "Please everybody, you must all try to remain calm," the stewardess shouted to make herself heard above the shrieks and screaming of the frenzied, panic stricken passengers.

"Listen to me, as soon as we are safely down you must leave the plane by the emergency exits here at the centre of the aircraft". She pointed to the doors.

In a desperate attempt to make light of the terrifying predicament they were in, Peter whispered to Bob sitting beside him. "I hope it doesn't mean that you will be needing crutches when we get out of this."

Bob gave him a forced grin, before they were suddenly plunged into darkness when the lights went out and the plane thundered down. Crashing into the thick blanket of snow covered ground that softened, and gradually eased their emergency landing as the wrecked remains of the aircraft came to a slithering, skidding halt.

All Bob could hear were the moans and groans coming from the injured people then all became silent.

Most of the villagers in the small community had heard the aircraft come screaming down, and had watched in horror as it hurtled through the forest trees to the ground below and ploughed into the deep snow, before disappearing from sight.

In no time at all, a group of men had rallied together to form a search party. They rapidly harnessed their horses to the sleds and were already on their way to the crash site, while others raced into the village to get help.

Bob, Peter, Janet and Sandra sat in the darkness too stunned to move, before Bob asked.

"Can you move? If so then we`d better get out of here before it catches fire,"

Despite their sprained limbs, and cuts and bruises, the four managed to loosen their seat belts and clambered from the plane, over the wreckage and luggage scattered about in the snow.

Bob, however, stood for a few moments before deciding that he was going back inside the wrecked fuselage to check if anyone was trapped and still alive. But doubted it when he saw the devastating carnage surrounding them.

"The stewardess was standing in the aisle trying to calm a woman when we came down so she could be hurt. Has anyone got a flashlight?"

"I have," Peter said, taking one from his pocket. "But it`s only small, I use it for reading on the flight so I don't disturb anyone who is sleeping"

He handed the torch over to Bob. "Thanks" Bob said and shone the small beam of light over the twisted metal remains of the devastated aircraft, wondering in disbelief how they had managed to survive the crash. The aircraft had been totally annihilated. He was sickened by what he saw and had to turn his head from the sight of mangled bodies, pierced by chunks of metal that had penetrated through them. Some were partially buried and scattered about in the snow while some were still fastened to the seats.

Shaking from the cold and shock, Bob faced his friends, "The engines must have dropped off somewhere else before we hit the ground, or we would have been goners if the plane had caught fire." His voice trembled as he spoke.

"I`d better get back in there and see if anybody else is alive."

Bob climbed into what was left of the aircraft and shone the light around, but all he could could see were more mangled bodies trapped in the wreckage. The stewardess had been thrown towards the front of the aircraft where she lay with her inners slashed wide open and her legs twisted at peculiar angles, while her arms and other body parts were missing .

Forcing himself to look away from the nauseating sight, Bob managed to struggle over sharp chunks of twisted wreckage to reach the cockpit, where he found the pilot and co- pilot, dead, with sharp shards of shattered glass and metal protruding through their inert bodies.

The sight was too much for Bob; he threw up, then wiped his mouth on his sleeve. He struggled back to the others who were stood waiting anxiously for his return.

"They`re all dead. It looks as if we were the lucky ones being seated at the centre of the Aircraft. It is just a tangled mess inside." Was all he managed to say before succumbing to the emotion he was feeling, and broke down sobbing.

"I guess we had better look for shelter`" Peter`s teeth chattered as he spoke.

"The weather is getting worse and it`s getting colder by the minute , so I suggest that we get moving before we all freeze to death."

"There are lights over there," Sandra said pointing towards an isolated property. "It looks like a big house," Peter agreed, squinting through the curtain of snow.

"Never mind what it is, it will mean shelter. Come on, let`s get moving". Peter, who had lost his crutches in the crash, had to be helped as they struggled through the deep snow. Where upon reaching the old stone building they realised that it was a chateau, and hesitated not knowing what to do or say, before Bob picked up the courage to rap loudly on the door.

"Oh my goodness!" Janet exclaimed in shock, when a thin, gaunt man who appeared to be the butler opened the door, looked around then closed it in their faces.

"What the hell`s wrong with you, we need help our plane has crashed and we are freezing to death out here, for goodness sake let us in." Sandra yelled banging ferociously on the hard wooden door.

"Who is it Carlos?" they heard the frail voice on an elderly lady calling.

"Nobody mistress, there`s nobody there".

"Come, come, there has to be I distinctly heard someone knocking. Open the door and let me see who it is".

The heavy door creaked open allowing them to stumble inside, where they saw ornate flickering oil lamps lit the dark hallway, casting weird dancing shadows across the tapestries and family portraits that were hung on the stone and plaster covered walls.

" Oh my goodness," the lady exclaimed, when seeing the four bedraggled figures.

"Please help us" Sandra begged.

"We`ve just had a terrible accident and we are freezing cold"

"Where are your manners Carlos", come in, look at you all, you are soaking wet and need to dry out, come and sit by the fire".

"Gina" "Yes Contessa"

"Get something warm for these poor children to drink.

"Yes Contessa", Gina threw Carlos a confused glance.

"Have you noticed that most parts of the building are lit by oil lamps and candles?"

Sandra whispered to Bob.

"Well you can`t expect them to have electricity in such a remote area can you?" he whispered softly.

"It is a bit spooky though, don`t you think?"

Peter, who was peering through the stone mullion window, unexpectedly called out that there was a lot of movement at the crash site.

"I can see lanterns moving about but not much else, the snow is falling too heavily for me to see what`s going on".

Their conversation was interrupted by an unexpected constant knocking at the door.

"Carlos go see who it is"

"Yes Contessa"

Carlos opened the door and ushered three men into the great hall, where they stood respectfully with their caps in their hands in front of the lady.

"Now then, what is it all this noise about?, what can I do for you?"

"Contessa there has been a terrible accident in the valley".

"We saw a plane come down Contessa, it was near the Villa Rappatta. Just a few people who are still alive have already been taken to the hospital, but there are some unfortunate ones who didn't survive. We have come to ask if you would be gracious enough to allow us to bring the bodies here and put them in the empty stables until the authorities arrive to collect them tomorrow".

"It is not right that we leave them for the scavengers to devour, the wolves are already gathering in packs, and if we are not careful they will attack the horses. And we will be unable to recover the bodies if we wait much longer".

"Of course you can bring them here", she replied I will have Carlos unlock the empty stables and he will be waiting there for you".

"Bless you, you are a very kind and gracious lady Contessa". All three men respectfully backed and bowed as they slowly retreated from the great hall.

"She must be someone of importance," Sandra said keeping her voice low.

"Did you notice how they spoke so respectfully to her?"

"Yes," Peter replied, although his thoughts were elsewhere at that moment. After a time they could hear the bells jingling from the horse harnesses as they slowly made their way through the drifting snow and into the courtyard.

"Gina," the Contessa called.

"Could you go through the back way and give the men sheets to cover those poor unfortunate people"

Gina nodded to the Contessa and left the room.

"I think we should go and help," Bob suggested to Peter.

Peter nodded in agreement, and followed Bob down the long passage leading to the stables adjoining the building. They watched as the solemn procession entered the stable and carefully laid the corpses side by side on the cold flagged floor.

By now the Contessa was by their side and gazing sorrowfully down at the victim`s bodies.

"It is such a shame they were so young," one man said, shaking his head.

"Yes, so young and as so pretty" she agreed, nodding sympathetically as she gently wiped a wisp of hair from one of the dead girls faces.

"It will be such a terrible loss for their parents". The Contessa suddenly turned pale when glancing at the dead girl, then gave a slight gasp and collapsed onto a heap on the floor.

One of the rescuers rushed to her side and lifted her into a sitting position and began gently tapping her cheeks until she recovered slightly.

"What is it, what is wrong Contessa?" he asked in concern.

She groaned weekly and pointed into one of the stalls before relapsing into an unconscious state.

"Mama Mia" said one, and crossed himself as he muttered something to the others, that caused them to turn and run.

Then pushing all etiquette to one side, he lifted the Contessa and raced along the corridor into the lounge and placed her on the sofa, before scurrying away.

"What on earth is wrong with them?", Bob exclaimed.

Then stopped when seeing Peter and Janet standing beside them.

"What are you two doing here? I thought you were staying in the lounge?" he asked.

"We were, but for some strange reason we felt compelled to come here."

All of a sudden, the whole area became icy cold and bore a weird sense of ethereal reality . "I don`t like this" Janet voiced.

"Something is wrong, it must be with being with them," she pointed to the covered bodies. "Let`s get out of here".

"Just a minute, I want to see what upset the old lady so much. She was looking at one of the bodies, then passed out," Bob murmured quietly, pulling back the sheet covering one of the corpse.

"Oh my god!" he gasped as he went from one body to the other pulling back the sheets. "What is it? What`s wrong?" Sandra asked.

"Never mind what`s wrong just get over here and look I know it`s not a pretty sight, but you might as well know what upset the Contessa". Sandra, Janet and Bob hesitantly made their way over to where Peter was standing and stared down in shock at the gruesome sight of their own mutilated bodies lying there.

They then realised that they were dead, and the Contessa was the only person capable of seeing them.

BOGGLE HOLE, ROBIN HOOD`S BAY, EAST YORKSHIRE

"What a change after all of the rain we`ve been having," Sue said to herself when she awoke and noticed the brilliant sunlight streaming in through the gap of the curtains of her bedroom window.

Rubbing the sleep from her eyes she sat up and shivered from the cold of the early winter morning. But as soon as her feet touched the carpet on the wooden floor of her cottage, she pulled them back under the bedcovers and huddled there for a while until she felt the warmth of the cosy fluffy blankets seeping through her.

Nevertheless, she knew that she had to get out of bed as Millie her dog, needed her early morning walk and was already scratching at the bedroom door, ready and waiting to be on the way for her regular constitutional.

Boggle Hole, situated near Robin Hood`s Bay in East Yorkshire, was where Sue lived alone after the premature death of her husband Michael, she always found a comforting sense of peace when walking along that lonely stretch of beach where she and Michael had walked only a few months previously. They would stand and watch the heavy, rolling waves breaking and crashing with a thunderous roar, over the rocks, before subsiding and swirling towards the sandy shore.

Sue always found that Boggle Hole was a most pleasant and peaceful area in the winter months, especially when the tourists had returned home, far away from the cold, harsh blustery winds and storms.

Pushing the past sad memories behind her, Sue had forced herself out of her warm comfy bed, dressed had breakfast and then fed Millie.

Next she slipped into her thermal waterproofs that would protect her from the cold, blustery winds, and pulled on her thick socks and galoshes. Then she went outside to the car to take the short drive to Boggle Hole.

Upon their arrival, Sue let Millie loose on the beach where she went bounding off barking and chasing seagulls who were busy pecking at the seaweed, sending them screeching angrily as they flew up into the sky away from Millie's yapping jaws.

Sue smiled as she watched the dog's antics for a few moments before Millie bound off to find something new to investigate, while Sue walked along the beach searching for different fossils to add to her collection. She was also grateful that as winter was fast approaching, there were no tourists on the beach to distract her, and she enjoyed having the space to herself.

Apart from seeing the occasional neighbour who was out walking their dogs, Sue had found herself alone most of the time on the vast stretch of beach. She had discovered a number of fossils that she could add to her collection, and had placed them into the carrier bag she had taken with her. These had fallen from the cliff face after it had collapsed, when the lower areas of unstable sections of land had been swept away by the incoming tides.

By now, the wind was howling around her and was almost knocking her from her feet as she systematically searched and dug with her trowel through the gritty patches of sand for the half- buried fossils. She was also thankful that she had chosen the close- fitting woolly hat that she had recently bought to keep her head warm beneath the hood of her jacket, as it was now beginning to spatter with sleet and icy rain.

As she scrambled over a clump of large rocks that were retaining pools of water, Sue noticed a number of small crabs hiding beneath the huge chunks of seaweed that had gathered there, and were struggling to escape from the screeching gulls' ferocious attacks.

Sue couldn`t bear the thought of the water draining away from their only source of protection and the tiny creatures being left to the mercy of the gulls.

So she lifted the tiny creatures out of their confined spaces and placed them, squirming into the bag, and carried them to where the waves were trickling along the shore. Then released them into the water where they disappeared beneath the rolling waves.

"Now that`s what I call being sociable," she heard a man say.

Sue jumped at the sound of his voice and turned.

She was surprised to see that a couple with a young boy had been watching her.

"I`m sorry, but do I know you?" she stammered, wiping her dripping wet hands down her jacket.

"I`m Sue Wilsons, I live close by here, I`m collecting fossils with my dog"

`What the hell am I garbling about?` she thought to herself.

The man smiled as he watched her cheeks flush with embarrassment. "I`m Bernard Harris, this is my wife Jenny and our son Tristan". He held out his hand as he introduced them, then pointed towards a large old house situated away from the cliff edge.

"We have lived there for the past eight years," he told her.

"It was so quiet and peaceful when we first visited the area that we decided that we wanted to stay, and after looking around at numerous properties we bought that house."

"It`s just far enough away from the cliffs for us not to be concerned about coastal erosion."

"The only drawback though is the noise and bad behaviour from the rowdy holiday makers who converge here in the summer months. We do manage to escape however on our boat that we keep moored at the marina for the winter. We spend a lot of time on it when the winter is over and do a spot of fishing. So why don`t you join us sometime?. You can bring the dog` it will be company for Tristan". "I`d love to," Sue replied.

"But are you sure about Millie, she is a big dog?".

"It`s a big boat," he replied.

"What do you and your husband do in the summer? Have you any children?" Jenny asked, smiling.

"My husband died six months ago, and we have no children." "Oh, I am sorry".

"Don`t be sorry, we had five wonderful years together before he was killed in a car crash he was only twenty eight, but we had known one another from childhood."

"Well, would you like to walk with us?" Bernard asked interrupting before Jenny could ask any more personal questions.

Sue glanced around searching for Millie, and saw Tristan running behind her waving his arms in the air, as together they chased the screeching gulls along the beach.

"It would be nice to have some company for a change," she added, with a smile as Jenny linked arms and proceeded to walk with her across the wet sand that squelched underfoot with each step they took.

"The weather`s turned bad again, and the sea`s getting rougher" Nelly Williams grumbled to her husband Fred, as they stood watching from the window of their bungalow when the storm finally broke. Lightning flashed across the sky, followed by continuous rumbling bouts of thunder. All of a sudden, gale force winds arose, sending hail and snow rattling across the windows of their home, forcing them back to the comforting warmth of their glowing fire.

Fred handed Nellie a pot of tea he had just brewed and sat down in the chair opposite her.

"If I recall, it was on a day like this when that family and the young widow with her dog got washed out to sea in that chap`s boat," he said with a sigh.

"I do remember that", Nelly expressed shaking her head sadly. "They never did find any trace of them, did they?" "No," he replied.

"And they can`t get anybody to stay in that cottage either, they say she and her dog haunts it.

SERENA

"That cat has to go,"
George glanced up from the newspaper he was reading,
"What?" "I said, that cat has to go. We should put poison down, then we will be rid of it once and for all". George was thoroughly fed up with his wife`s constant nagging about Sabrina, the cat from next door. "It is laid in the herbaceous border and is ruining my floral arrangements".

"For goodness sake can`t you leave the poor creature alone for once? it isn't doing any harm the animal is asleep".

"That`s not the point" she snapped peevishly, making for the open patio door.

"I`ll get rid of it, you just watch me".

George jumped up from his chair and ran after her, afraid of what she might do too the poor defenceless animal and called out as she raised her foot to either kick or stamp on Serena.

Serena, a beautiful white Persian cat who had been sleeping soundly, lifted her white fluffy pompom head and stared in disbelief through her sleepy, aquamarine eyes at the angry woman standing in front of her.

"Get out of my garden you, horrible creature;" she shrieked hysterically. "Go away"

The woman drew back her leg ready to kick the unsuspecting feline.

Serena knew that she had to escape, but how? behind her was a brick wall and thick shrubbery that she couldn't get through` she knew that she was trapped and now realised that she should never have chosen the sunniest spot in Sally`s garden in which to sleep.

She couldn't get past the infuriated woman so the only means of escape was to use her head and think that was when her quick-witted survival instinct took over.

Serena arched her back and let out a deep threatening growl that emanated from the depths of her throat and she became a hissing mass of pure hatred at the vicious woman. Who's semblance was more akin to a troll than a human being.

Sally had not expected Serena's violent reaction and for a split second, the element of surprise took her off guard. Within that one split second however, Serena launched herself at Sally's thigh and dug her claws into the woman's fat, fleshy leg and hung on with all her might. Sally screamed in pain and stood flailing her arms wildly into the air as the sudden shock and pain shot through her.

"George, George!" she screamed, not daring to move.

"Get this thing off me".

Serena held on, revelling in the pain she was causing. However when she heard the sound of George's heavy footsteps approaching and the clunk of his walking stick, Serena decided that it was time to retreat and get away from there.

With a final warning hiss, Serena let go and dropped to the ground, raced across the lawn, then squeezed through a gap in the hedge bottom to the safety of her own territory.

In the meantime, Joanna, Serena's owner, had rushed into the garden to see what all the fuss was about and had to duck when a barrage of stone missiles shot over the hedge towards her.

"Stop that, you moronic imbecile, have you gone completely mad?" Joanna shouted at the top of her voice.

For a brief moment everything went quiet in the next door garden.

"Stop prodding me," she heard George hiss.

"It wasn't doing any harm, for goodness sake woman, it was asleep until you kicked it".

"Tell her, tell her," she heard Sally whisper in a loud angry tone.

"No, you tell her, it was you the cat scratched not me,"

"I have told you before to speak to her about that creature, I don`t want it in my garden it kills my plants"

"Oh, for goodness sake" he whined.

Joanna had to stifle a grin when George`s harassed face appeared over the hedge` he always had the ridiculous habit of giving a nervous cough and supporting his glasses with a finger that threatened to slide down his nose whenever Sally forced him to do something he didn't want to do.

He coughed again then spoke in his usual whimpering voice.

"I`m sorry to have to tell you this Joanna, but your cat has just scratched my wife"

"Get out of the way George, let me speak to her".

Sally`s puffy fat face appeared beside him. "That cat of yours has attacked me. It ought to be put down you should see my leg. If I get blood poisoning then it will be your fault and I will sue you" she shrieked loudly enough for the whole street to hear.

With that, Joanna`s patience ran out.

"I would rather see you put down, you, nasty woman", Joanna retorted angrily.

"Nobody in this street likes you because of your nasty ways and evil tongue, and I promise you this, if you throw stones at me or Serena ever again then I shall call the police. Do I make myself clear?".

Shaking with anger, she picked up Serena and marched into her house leaving Sally gaping open-mouthed and silent. Nothing more was said of the incident until a few weeks later when George called round to let her know that Sally had died unexpectedly, and to invite her to the funeral.

"I am so sorry," she said, ushering him inside, "I didn't know, what happened?" Joanna asked.

"On Saturday afternoon at five o`clock, Sally fell in the garden. Her sister, Elizabeth was `with us when it happened.

We both thought that she was just a bit shaken because of the fall, but when she suddenly became pale and started sweating I called for an ambulance. But it was too late within minutes she had a massive heart attack and died".

"She did say before she died, that Sabrina had tripped her up on the lawn when she went to shoo her away from the flowers".

"But she couldn't have", Joanna said tearfully.

"Sabrina died while she was laying on my knee at exactly four o` clock Saturday afternoon".

RABBITS, RABBITS, RABBITS

The sun shone down brightly through the thick foliage of the budding leaves of the trees, spreading a wide spectrum of rays through the gaps where the branches met, thus creating a magical, concave canopy of entwining branches overhead.

Below, the partially open buds of the wildflowers were growing amongst the long blades of grass, where some had already burst through the soil to create a kaleidoscope carpet of colour.

Bluebells, daisies, cornflower and many other species of nature were already shooting from the ground and blooming amidst the dead foliage of yesteryear.

This miracle of beauteous nature however, was marred by the distant sounds of gunshots from the hunters` guns as they surged ahead, seeking to kill any sign of wildlife that existed in the forest.

"I wish I hadn't come," Bill moaned, as he stumbled through the knee- high bracken and automatically ducked his head as the sound of a rapid succession of gunfire reverberated from every angle around him.

"Shut up and keep your eye on that idiot over there, it`s the boss's son" David hissed.

"We don't want the bloody fool shooting us as he`s the one who winged one of the beaters yesterday".

"I know that, that`s the reason why I didn't want to come today," Bill replied testily, "but we all heard what the boss said".

Bill spoke in a sarcastic tone, mimicking his employer. "It is in the interest of you, the employees of this company, to volunteer and comply with whatever recreation our business clientele wish to partake in"

The thud and splatter of lead pellets hitting the tree directly alongside them sent both men plummeting to the ground for cover.

"I don`t believe it, what the bloody hell is that moron playing at?" David seethed.

"I don't know, but I`m staying put until that idiot is out of range, and I think you should do the same," Bill whispered.

For a long while they lay motionless and silent, hardly daring to breath, until the resounding volley of shots passed by and were gradually fading away into the far distance.

"That's it, I`ve had enough," Bill raged, clambering to his feet and dusting himself down.

"I`m going back to the clubhouse. I told you before we set off that I don't approve of blood sport.

Clay pigeon shooting I can cope with, but not this,"

"Shush, be quiet" Dave whispered. "Look over there by that tree"

Bill glanced over to where his friend was pointing and watched as a chubby white hare that had struggled through the long grass was now resting against a tree gasping for breath.

"This is the break you`ve been waiting for," David hissed.

"Shoot it you can`t miss from here. Hurry up, shoot it before it senses us and runs,"

Bill raised the gun to his shoulder but his hands were shaking so badly that he couldn't get his bearings.

"I can`t do it," Bill snapped angered by David`s persistent badgering and lowered the gun.

"For goodness sake it`s only a lousy hare" David snapped, "You have to start sometime"

"No, I can`t and I won`t do it," Bill retorted angrily

"It`s just an innocent little creature that isn't hurting anyone, and it deserves to live,"

"For goodness sake, what do you think people are going to say when we get back to the clubhouse?" David griped.

"Nobody will know if you keep your mouth shut," Bill snapped back.

Unnoticed by them, as they stood arguing, the hare had backed itself up onto its hind legs and was tearing at its chest in desperation, shouting.

"Don`t shoot, don`t shoot."

Mystified, the men watched in amazement as a little elf struggled out of the hare`s suit screaming, "It`s only a costume, don`t you know what day this is?"

They looked at one another, then back at the elf with a blank expression on their faces.

Tutting and shaking his head the little elf informed them, "It is the first day of March, and it is good luck to say` rabbits, rabbits, rabbits`, three times".

"Well, as it is the first day of March, we, the little people, celebrate with a fancy dress party and I am on my way to that party".

"This is my costume and I am the guest of honour; I am the lucky March hare".

Stuttering their apologies, Bill and David wished him luck and as they made their way back to the club house, they decided that it would be in their best interest if they didn't say anything about the hare, nor the elf. Otherwise they would have made a laughingstock of themselves. But as soon as they were out of sight, the little elf began laughing so much that he could hardly stand.

"Oh dear" he chortled

"These humans are so stupid, they don`t understand, that the white hare is a magical creature that can resume any form it chooses on the first day of March."

After giving a quick glance around him to ensure that no one was watching, the little elf clicked his finger, resumed his shape, and hopped safely away.

MY HARRY

It still makes me smile when people refer to me as the sweet little old lady down the lane. Perhaps it is because I make everyone welcome who comes to my door, and invite them in for a cup of tea and a biscuit. Or when a new neighbour moves in down the road, I always welcome them by doing a bit of baking for them.

But there I go again my Harry would put his arms around me and say that I was blowing my own trumpet. (That means bragging) if you don't understand Yorkshire.

I love people, it doesn't matter what or who they are, we are all cast in the same mould.

It's just that some are better or worse off than the rest of us. I don't tell anyone this but I am very lonely. At times I feel worthless and no use to anyone.

Nevertheless, whenever a new baby is due I am always the first person who is sent for.

What do you think of him, or her, granny? they ask; most people call me granny.

I always tell them how lucky they are, and that it is another bundle of joy sent from heaven, and I do mean it, some of them don't realise just how lucky they really are.

Today I got knocked down by a car. It's because I can't see properly, you understand.

It's not that I am careless, but there is such a lot of traffic, and bad impatient drivers who drive too fast, they don't give us' old uns' time to cross the road.

Anyway people do fuss and I soon had a crowd round helping me. Eee I was so embarrassed, sat there in the middle of the road. But some kind person picked me up and another brought a chair from a shop for me to sit on.

Well, the next thing I knew there was a police car and two bobbies asking if I was alright and saying they should take me to the hospital for a check- up. But I refused to go and it took a while for me to convince them that I was fine.

So they offered to drive me home, but the strange thing was that I couldn't remember my name or where I lived. It`s my age you know, you get like this with the years piling on. Then they asked the people in the crowd if anyone knew me, but nobody did.

So as I had refused to go to the hospital they took me to the police station instead.

I have never been in one of those places before and you mark my words, it was frightening.

But I need not have worried, a friendly police woman took me to a room on one side of the hall. It had a big window and I could see all that was happening. Well, the police lady brought me a cup of tea and some biscuits, and told me that they were making some enquiries to see if they could find out who I was. We even went through my handbag together to see if I had any identification in it, but I didn't. She said not to worry, someone was bound to miss me.

There was one thing though that I could remember, and that was I enjoyed writing poetry, So when I asked for a pen and paper just to help pass the time, it was soon arranged for me. A young woman with a sweet smile brought them, she was ever so pleasant and stopped to talk for a while, and before she left she said that if I needed anything I only had to ask.

Wasn't that kind.

Everything here is painted the same colour and I don't like it, it is too bright.

They brought some strange people in from time to time; some were shouting and swearing, while others were crying, and believe me, this will shock you, drunk, yes drunk, and it was still daytime. Well they say it takes all kinds to make the world go around. Ooh it is a busy place this, one of the ladies that was brought in by a policeman came up to me and asked.

"What have they nicked you for granny? Shoplifting or vagrancy?" I was very shocked and upset by her attitude, and when she realised what she had done, she said. "Sorry, luv, I was only joking". and came and put her arm around me. I told her that I was lost and couldn't remember my name and she was very sympathetic.

But while we were talking a policeman grabbed her arm and took her away, I didn't want her to go, because she did smell nice.

I can't help but think about my family, I had known love for just over 60 years, my Harry and I had been very happy. We'd had two wonderful children, but one of them died when she was only ten. Losing a child is hard, it is something that you never get over.

As the years have crept by I still find myself weeping over our beautiful lost child. Our other daughter grew up and moved far away to another country. She knew I would refuse when she asked me to go with them, but I didn't want to leave England because all of my happy memories are here, and I didn't really feel that they wanted me. I felt as if would have been in their way they had their own lives to live just as I've had mine.

Oh I wish I could remember my name.

My Harry had worried about me just before he died, he held my hand and said with tears in his eyes. "Who's going to look after you love with me gone". I patted his hand and said, "don't worry about me love I have my little shop, I'll get by". And I did, I did quite nicely for myself.

I remember our daughter saying shortly before she left, "I know I won't have to worry about you mum, you are so confident and independent, I know that you will be alright".

She left me with a hug and a kiss and dry eyes. I'll never forget that moment when she boarded that airplane, and when that plane took off, with her went the rest of my life. She will never know that to this day, that was when my heart finally broke and I felt truly alone. I shed tears for days, lots of them, but then as Harry would say. Come on lass pull thee socks up and get on with it.

I feel so tired. These kind people keep coming and asking If I am alright, and I tell them Yes"

But although I have my memories I still can`t remember my name, and I am feeling a little strange. Perhaps it could be a bit of shock from earlier on, I don`t really know. The bright lights shining on the white walls are making my eyes ache, so I think I shall have to ask if they can turn them down a bit, but I can`t do that can I?. It would be bad manners after all they have done for me, and I don't want to sound like an old grouch.

Anyway, my eyes are always playing tricks on me and I see things that aren't really there and I walk into things and fall over them. The doctor said that it is cataracts and there is nothing they can do. I am too old for surgery. I am eighty six. It keeps growing darker, one minute I am seeing everything too bright and then it starts to go dark. I think there is someone in the room with me, I never heard them come in. I suppose it is more tea and biscuits. I can`t quite make out who it is. Now where did I put my glasses?. I took them off after I had written my poem so that I could rest my head onto my arms over the table and I closed my eyes for a while, Now I can`t find my glasses. Can you come closer? I can`t see you properly Oh I can`t believe it, not after all these years.

Harry, my Harry, but what are you doing here. Did you get run over as well?.

I can see him clearly now and he is smiling, and my eyes have stopped hurting.

Why, he is holding out his arms to me, I must go to him.

Oh Harry, you don`t know how long I have waited for this moment. Don`t leave me again, please don`t leave me, I love you so much that it hurts and it is making my heart ache for you.

Listen, he is telling me that he will wait, but first I must finish off what I am doing.

I look down and there is the pen in my hand and the paper is filled with my writing, but I didn't realise I was doing it. I wonder if I have been writing down what I was thinking of just now. Harry, I don`t want to write anymore I want to be with you.

He is telling me that I must thank everyone for helping me before I go, so I write.

I truly and sincerely thank you for all the help that you have to give me when I needed it, but I must tell you this. I am grateful to have known both sadness and joy, for without sadness I would never have known what true joy really is.

I want you to understand that. Whenever there are tears and harsh words between you and your loved one, always make up before going to sleep, you never know if one of you will never wake again. Or if you are going off to work, kiss and make up, you never know it could be the last time you ever see or speak to one another.

Most of all, don`t be afraid to love, for to love and be loved is the most important thing in the world.

I must go now Harry is waiting for me. Oh it is wonderful to feel his arms about me, I feel so safe and secure, He is taking me with him.

Goodbye everybody, goodbye.

PC Christine Barker entered the room and noticed that the elderly lady was laid with her arms spread across the table and immediately knew that something was wrong. She sent for the prison doctor who sadly declared her dead on examination.

After she had been removed from the small but comfortable room, Christine picked up the papers the lady had been writing on and wept as she read.

TO LOVE AND BE LOVED

To love and be loved, who could ask for anything more.

To be with the one who cares for me, whom I worship and adore.

To feel your arms around me, when I`m sad you hold me tight.

I feel your strength and manliness, and then I am alright.

I love to see your happy smile it brightens up my day.

Just being here together, what more do I need to say?.

We will stay together, after all that we`ve been through.

I know that you belong to me and I belong to you.

Poem by Elisa Wilkinson

THE FLORAL ARRANGEMENT

"Oh dear where do I start," Allison groaned looking helplessly about the old church. "I've never set the church up for a wedding before, it's always been for a funeral".

"You need a white rose, with a little greenery tied with pretty ribbons, set at the top side corner of each alternate pew leading up to the alter".

Allison turned and was surprised to see an attractive, good looking young woman standing behind her, wearing a pretty pink, floral summer dress, and medium high heeled shoes. Her long auburn hair cascaded down her back almost to her waist, and her twinkling blue eyes held a hint of mischief.

"Oh, for a minute there you scared me, I thought I was alone in the church".

"No, I'm usually about to lend a helping hand when it comes to weddings, You could place a circular floral bouquet resting on the top of each of the tall urns on either side of the alter with ribbons and greenery draped over the sides," she suggested.

"Oh, by the way I'd better introduce myself, I'm Carol" she broke off in mid-sentence when David Clarke, the elderly verger, entered the church with a group of people.

"I will speak to you later, he's giving one of his tours," Carol whispered in hushed tones and hurried away into the dark recess of the church towards the rear exit.

The verger made his apologies to the people he had been speaking to before making his way towards Allison.

"Yours was the only florist in the neighbourhood that wasn't closed this week, our usual florist appears to be away on holiday," he grumbled wringing his hands in frustration. "I was just giving these people a guided tour of the church, so if you wouldn't mind keeping out of the way," he waved his hand in their direction.

"I will get back to them and continue the tour."

"Thanks for the compliment you, ignorant old sod", she mumbled softly to herself then said loudly.

" I thought for a moment there, you were going to say that you had chosen me because of my faultless flower arrangements."

For a moment David was taken by surprise by her reaction and backed away when feeling his face turning a brilliant red.

"I`m sorry, I didn`t mean it to sound that way, weddings always do this to me." With a look of total dismay on his face, David scurried back to the group who were pointing out features in the carved monolithic stone to one another.

"Thank-goodness he`s gone," Allison muttered to herself returning to what she was doing.

"Have they gone?" she heard someone say behind her. "Who?" Allison spun round to see who was speaking.

"Oh it`s you" "Yes it`s me" Carol said with a big smile.

"Oh no, here comes the groom," Carol`s face suddenly took on a look of complete hatred.

Allison glanced over to the doorway where she could see a tall good looking man dressed casually in jeans and a pale blue shirt, enter the church who was standing in the vestry doorway.

"Wow, he`s a bit of alright" Allison whispered to Carol.

"Don`t be taken in by his good looks and charm, that gigolo was never entirely cleared of the murder of his wife and baby daughter three years ago. Everyone in the village knew that he never wanted children, and he was having an affair with two other women when they died. The whole community believe that he had something to do with their deaths, and so do the police, but it`s a matter of proving it. One of his mistresses however, gave him a strong alibi by claiming that he was with her at the time of his family`s deaths. Now he`s marrying Gillian Cartage, a different one, she is rich and can afford to keep him in the manner he has grown accustomed to. I`d better be going" she said, glancing towards him.

"I don`t want him to see me talking to you".

Carol hurried away once again towards the rear exit: she didn`t want to be anywhere near Alec Elliot as he nonchalantly made his way towards Allison.

"I have decided to place a white rose tied with ribbon on each alternate pew" she began, but was immediately stopped from saying anymore.

"No" Alec snapped in a voice like thunder and a violent look on his face.

"No` No` No", he slammed his hand down hard on the side of the font near where they were standing. "What have I said? What is wrong?" she cried jumping back in alarm.

It took Alec a few minutes to regain his composure. "I`m sorry, I shouldn't have spoken to you like that, it`s just that, it was what my first wife chose when we were married here."

"Oh, I`m sorry, I didn`t know, don`t worry about it I can create another arrangement just as easily." "Thanks" he replied curtly, and left her staring after him as he walked over to the door and left the church.

The big day was soured for Alec and his new bride to be when they crossed the Graveyard and an ominous black cloud floated across what had been a bright sunny sky, plummeting everything into darkness and bringing with it a gloomy portent.

Everyone stopped moving and waited. In a matter of minutes all of the happy chatter and laughter had ceased when hearing Alec cry out in alarm as he fell across a grave. Gillian, then let out a terrified scream as she fell onto the grave beside Alec in a dead faint.

Unnoticed by anyone standing there, a hand had reached up from beneath the soil and grabbed Alec by the ankle forcing him to the ground. When Gillian had reached down to him to find out what was wrong, a tiny ice -cold hand had taken hold of hers, forcing her face forward onto the grave alongside Alec.

The local doctor, who had been invited to the wedding, had hurried over to the stricken couple to see if he could help. But when he checked them both neither had a pulse and were pronounced dead.

Therefore, there was no wedding, but the sun came out and the birds sang once more, and the disappointed guests left for home.

Allison could not believe what had happened and sadly made her way into the church where she dropped into a pew. And with tears cascading down her face she sat staring at all of her beautiful flower arrangements .

"It is sad to say that nobody liked him," she heard the Verger say as he slipped into the pew beside her.

"This is a photo of him with his first wife Carol Davis".

David handed her a picture that he had removed from the board in the church.

"She was a lovely kind- hearted girl. Everybody knew that he had killed her but they couldn't prove anything, but we all knew that he had fixed the brakes on her car that had killed her and their daughter, Suzy.

Allison glanced down at the picture he was holding and gasped.

"That was the young woman who helped me with the floral arrangements. She wanted me to place a single white rose on every alternate pew, but Alec told me not to do that. Now I understand why he wanted something different.

"Yes, and where he and Gillian died, was on the grave where Carol and his daughter are buried".

JACK

"How much is it Jack?"

"Two pounds, Jack replied holding out his hand for the money.

"Councils are putting prices up soon on all car parks"

"Bloody hell, the greedy bastards." Brian cursed.

"As if they don`t take enough from us with the bloody Council Tax" he grumbled getting, into his car and driving away.

Jack shook his head sadly as he walked back to his tiny shed and put the barrier down, knowing that the day would come when he they would be putting machines on his car park` then he would be out of a job.

The horn of an impatient driver sent him scurrying from his hut to the car, and bent down beside the driver`s window.

"How much?," the driver snapped, impatient to be on his away as he handed Jack the ticket.

Jack knew that the man was aware of how long he had been parked, nevertheless he made a show of checking the time on the ticket.

"Three fifty," he said, holding out his hand.

"Three fifty?" the man snapped in a raised tone.

"That`s daylight robbery."

Jack waved the parking document under his nose.

"You've been parked here for three and a half hours, and it`s not me who sets the charges, it's the bloody council."

The disgruntled man reached into his pocket for some change and paid for the allotted time then drove away in a fury.

"He`s in a bloody rush," Jack mumbled, as he went to the next car.

Just then an harassed and angry man dashed across the car park. "Has a bloke in a green Jaguar been parked here?" he shouted.

Jack turned round and looked behind him unsure if the man was speaking to him or not.

"You! Yes you, you, scruffy bloody idiot," he yelled, pointing at Jack.

Jack felt his hackles rising` he didn`t like being called names, especially being referred to as a scruffy bloody idiot, and ignored him.

"I`m talking to you, you fucking moron!" he shouted.

Jack turned a deaf ear to the verbal abuse and carried on collecting money from the drivers as they left the car park. He then returned to his shed, closed the lower half of the door and set about making himself a pot of tea on his paraffin stove that he had bought from the second-hand shop in town.

Jack began to wonder if it was his appearance that made so many people angry. Granted he needed a haircut and only shaved twice a week, but his working clothes were good as they came from the local charity shop. He also knew that he stank. Nevertheless he paid his hard-earned money and showered once a week at the filling station where the truckers got cleaned up.

By now however, the man`s rage had diminished slightly and he had managed to calm himself down, as he approached Jack in a more polite and civilised manner.

"Look, I`m sorry about the way I spoke to you earlier, but It`s just that I`m a bit upset."

He rubbed his head in frustration while Jack waited for an explanation.

"Well, I caught my wife in compromising position in my own home with another man". The poor soul appeared to be so distraught and upset that Jack began to feel sorry for him.

"Tell you what, here" Jack picked up his pen and scribbled something down on a scrap of paper and handed it to the distressed man.

The man in turn read it, then gave him a huge smile of gratitude as he reached into his pocket and handed Jack a tenner before dashing away in the direction he had come from.

`Well, that was easy money,` Jack thought as he cheerfully kissed the note and pushed it into the money bag that he kept strapped around his waist.

It was the best decision he ever made, when he decided to always make a note of the licence plate and make of car that was on his car park, just in case somebody became awkward about the parking fee and tried to drive away without paying. He was also terrified that someone would try to rob him, so he always banked the money after finishing work.

Autumn came and went and in no time at all winter had arrived, Jack had spent the last eleven years of his life on the car park, and his regular clients had come to regard him more as a friend than a council employee.

After the Christmas season was over and life had returned to normal, no one could get onto the car park as barriers had been placed at the entrance and Jack was missing.

Whereby many of his regular customers became concerned for his wellbeing, and had contacted the council in order to check up on his whereabouts.

To the council`s amazement, they discovered that they didn't know that they owned the patch of land that was habitually used as a car park, and after thoroughly checking their list of employees working regularly on every car park in that area, they couldn't find any trace of a Jack Burrows.

Even when the police were called to investigate, no one could find him. In time, as far as everyone was concerned Jack Burrows had never existed.

In the peace, and sunshine of the Bahamas, Jim Barlow, alias (Jack Burrows), was at last living the life style about which he had always dreamt of. He was surrounded by pretty girls, had a nice chilled drink in his hand from the beach bar that he owned on the sunny Caribbean island, and there was a cool, balmy breeze whispering softly around him.

Jim smiled to himself, knowing that he was safely away from the authorities who had given him up for dead. There would be no more freezing cold winters on that car park, or any other, in the foreseeable future.

THE ROSE GARDEN

"He`s back." "Who`s back?"

"Steve Parker, the market gardener, his muddy work boots were on the step next door again when I drove past."

"Don`t you have anything better to do than pry into other people`s business?" Dennis Green snapped at his wife, Elaine.

"No I don`t," Elaine snapped back

"Not when he is a married man with three young children. What if he catches something from her that he can`t get rid of?."

"For goodness sake, Elaine."

"Somebody should tell his wife."

"Well, it`s not going to be you, just stay out of it and keep your mouth shut. We don`t want you bringing any trouble here."

"Huh," Elaine mumbled to herself as she went into the kitchen to empty the shopping from the bags she had brought home.

Everybody in the avenue knew that the woman, Amy Townsend, was easy with her favours and had low morals; no woman`s husband was safe, Elaine grumbled to herself.

She had even wondered at times what Dennis got up to when her back was turned. Nevertheless, a few days later, a neighbour Doreen Hunter, stopped Elaine in the street asking if she had heard about Sally and Ted Johnson.

"No," Elaine replied, but from the look on Doreen`s face and the tone in her voice, Elaine immediately knew that something was wrong. "What is it? What`s happened?"

"Sally caught Ted with you know who."

"What?, No!" she exclaimed, shocked at what she was hearing.

"Ted thought Sally was at work, but she wasn't feeling too well and came home early." Doreen's voice had dropped to a dubious whisper.

"They were in Sally's bed, doing you know what."

"Oh my goodness, what did she do?"

"She rang her mother, packed her bags, took the car, picked the children up from school, and left him."

Elaine was so shocked she couldn't think of anything to say, until Doreen noticed a neighbour who had overheard what she'd said, and had dashed off to tell her friend the devastating news.

As soon as Elaine returned home she told Ted what Doreen had said.

"Get the facts straight before repeating what she told you, you know what a lying big mouthed gossip she is. Even her own husband says if she can't think of anything to gossip about she'll make it up, and drag anybody down to her own gutter level".

Elaine stood thinking for a while about what her husband had said` he was right of course, Doreen was known to be a liar as well as the local scandal monger. No one believed a word she said, especially when the person she was gossiping about was known to be a good upstanding person in the community, they took whatever she had to say with a pinch of salt.

Nevertheless, there had to be a small semblance of truth in what she was saying. Surely even she wouldn't dare go around telling a lie about something as terrible as she was now gossiping about.

Just then the phone rang. It was Hillary, Sally and Ted's next door neighbour asking if she had heard about Ted's misdemeanour.

"Yes", Elaine replied, Doreen is running around telling everybody who will listen.

"That bloody woman, she can't keep her big mouth shut for love nor money."

"I agree, but what can we do to help Sally?. She won't be able to face anyone right now, not after what that dirty bugger has done. He wants castrating."

"I'm with you on that, but we have to come up with a plan to help Sally. We can't even get rid of that bitch, she's having it off with a councillor."

"I know, I heard about that, and I've also seen them out together."

"I wonder if his wife knows or his regular mistress?" Elaine snorted with a sneering laugh.

"They won't be too happy about it will they, when they find out?."

"They will when they start scratching, wont they."

Hillary screeched with laughter at Hillary's comment.

"What do you say we get our heads together to decide on a plan of action to help Sally to get rid of the bugger, and get her back into her own home?" Elaine suggested with a hint of malevolence in her voice.

"Good idea, what about lunch on Wednesday at The Happy Tearooms?" Hillary suggested.

"Will you be able to get away for twelve thirty?. Maybe if we get our heads together we can somehow work out a solution to this problem, for Sally and the girls."

"Twelve thirty will be fine, Dennis will be at the golf club for most of the day, and so will your husband Brian."

"That's right, I forgot, they will be having lunch together and a few drinks. To be honest, it couldn't have been timed better," Hillary giggled mischievously.

"And I promise not to breathe a word to anyone about our plans." A few months passed and the gossip of Ted and Suzy's affair had died down. Sally was back home with the children and going about her usual routine.

As far as everyone knew, Ted had left the area, so had Amy Townsend, whereby everyone presumed that they had left together.

Elaine however, and Hillary, knew better. Steve Palmer wasn't leaving muddy boots on Amy's doorstep anymore, but he had planted Elaine a beautiful new rose garden, and after taking his advice, she had the best possible compost feeding them.

When she had asked Sam Palmer for his advice on what would be the best feed for the Roses, he had suggested that the plants always needed a good natural compost for healthy growth. He said that it should be well dug-in before the roses were planted.

After dosing their husbands` late night drinks with Elaine`s sleeping pills, Elaine and Hillary had toiled at midnight every night for almost a week, digging an area deep enough to accommodate the two unwanted decomposing bodies. They had been kept hidden behind the bushes, and were now beginning to create an unpleasant odour.

The stench of putrefaction had been replaced by the sweet scented rose garden that Elaine had named May Dante, and no one suspected a thing.

THE CAR

Smugness and self-gratification filled Kerry with pride as he laid back languishing in the elegant, sporty new vehicle he had purchased bearing his own initials KEH 1.

Seated behind the wood and chrome racing wheel bearing the Jaguar headed logo, he allowed his fingers to fondle and caress the soft cream leather upholstery, and felt slightly heady when smelling the newness of the vehicle.

It had taken him a considerable amount of hard work and time consuming effort to be able to afford his dream car, but he had finally achieved his goal, that was to say, with a little help from his father.

This was the car he had always dreamt of owning, a brannew, flame red, E-type Jaguar.

The smell of burning rubber filled the air as the screech of skidding tyres and heavy braking caused the bonnets of motorists' cars to dip when the drivers braked to avoid a collision.

The drivers behind watched horrified, as the car up ahead smashed against the crash barrier, then swerved from one lane to another narrowly missing other vehicles as it hurtled out of control along the motorway.

"God almighty, what's wrong with the dammed thing?" Elizabeth screamed as she desperately fought to bring her vehicle under control.

Luckily, she managed to slow down and direct the car onto the hard shoulder, and stopped wondering what the hell was wrong with it. Then to make matters worse, a police car with flashing lights had pulled up behind her and she watched as one of the officers got out of the car. "Oh no, now I'm for it," she moaned softly as in the rear-view mirror she saw him alight. then shrieked, when, staring back at her, was the mangled face of a blood-soaked man.

"I don't believe this is happening" she garbled to herself, thinking that due to the near miss, she was in a state of shock and having illusions. Giving a sigh of relief, she forced herself to turn and look in the back seat and could see quite clearly that no one was there, she was alone in the car.

"Thank God," she muttered to herself. Then screamed in terror, when after glancing into the rear view mirror again, she saw the same disfigured man sitting behind her.

In a blind panic, Elizabeth leapt from the car and ran screaming into the arms of the approaching police officer, babbling hysterically.

"Get that thing out of my car," she shrieked, "Keep it away from me."

"What thing?" Officer Evans asked puzzled by her odd behaviour.

"What are you talking about, there was only you in the car, come on I'll show you," he said trying to make light of her distress.

"No," she screamed, pulling away from his grasp.

"I won't ever go near that car again it's possessed it wants to kill me"

Officer Evans could see that the woman's fear was genuine and he turned to his colleague.

"Look after her Jack, while I take a look, I could have sworn she was on her own," he muttered, shaking his head.

Brian Evans strode over to the silver grey Jaguar and walked around it, peering inside at all angles, before calling to his colleague.

"There's nobody else in here Jack." Apart from the engine that was left running in Elizabeth's haste to escape, nothing else moved in the car. Brian opened the door and slid into the car and was about to switch off the engine, when at that precise moment, the door slammed shut and the central locking system thudded into place, trapping the officer inside.

"What the bloody hell's going on here?" he cursed, pulling at the door but it wouldn't open.

With a thunderous roar the powerful engine burst into life, throwing the startled officer back against the seat as it shot forward at an alarming speed.

Gritting his teeth and in mortal fear for his life, Brian grabbed hold of the steering wheel in an attempt to steer the car away from crashing into other traffic, as it careered madly swerving from one lane to another. He jammed his foot down hard onto the brake pedal but the car didn't respond.

At the same time, he reached out to switch off the engine, then recoiled in horror when a blood-soaked figure appeared beside him, that placed a crushed and bloody hand over his, preventing him from turning off the engine.

Brian couldn't utter a sound. The woman was right, the car was possessed.

"God give me strength," the officer whispered, as he glanced again at the ghastly creature seated beside him, and grimaced, sensing that he was about to die.

The man's shattered skull with one of its eyeballs missing turned towards him. "You can't escape. I couldn't. I'm so sorry," he heard the wraith utter softly.

Brian's blood ran cold when the car swung over into the third lane, and he sat paralysed with fear as he saw the parapet of a bridge looming directly in front of him.

In the final seconds of Officer Brian Evans life, he thought only of his family as he lapsed into unconsciousness screaming his wife's name, Dianna.

At the inquest three months later, Judge Heatherington found it hard to comprehend the hysterical woman's statement that the car was possessed and had been trying to kill her.

Nor could he understand why Officer Evans had locked himself in the car and had not tried to save himself.

Officer Jack Reed, had stated that Officer Evans had appeared to have fallen over towards the passenger seat when the car had taken off at high speed. Under those circumstances it was impossible for him to have been driving the car.

Also, when Officer Evans was being cut from the wreckage, he mumbled through his shattered jaw, that there was another person sitting beside him, who was already dead and had deliberately crashed the car. Yet no other person had been found in the mangled wreckage. Therefore the judge presumed that it must have been a figment of the officer`s confused mind as he died.

So was everyone hallucinating?.

At this point the judge sat shaking his head in disbelief.

However, another baffling factor arose. Officer Reed told them, that it had been discovered that the original owner of the Jaguar car had died after falling asleep at the wheel before crashing into the motorway bridge. For some strange reason it was the same bridge where Officer Evans had died.

Giving evidence, Elizabeth stated that she bought the car because of its registration bearing her Initials, Karen Elizabeth Holt. She had purchased it second-hand not knowing of its macabre history. If she had been made aware of the death of the past owner at the time, she said, then she would never have bought it.

The judge brought in a verdict of accidental death due to a mechanical malfunction of the car.

He didn't believe in haunted cars and ghosts.

Miss Brindle popped her head around the door of Judge Heatherington`s chambers.

"Your son Kerry Edwin is here in his new car and is waiting on the car park to take you home.

"Thank-you miss Brindle, tell him I`m on my way," the judge said, as he packed the final note he had made into his briefcase. Then after checking the desk to make sure he hadn't left anything of importance behind, he closed the door and left the building. "Come on dad, I have a surprise for you," Kerry greeted him with a big smile on his face.

My new car arrived today, and I wanted you to be the first person to try it out with me".

The judge smiled at his son's youthful enthusiasm as he steered him towards the brand new shining E type Jaguar.

But blanched when seeing the registration plate affixed to it.

"Where did you get that registration plate from?" he held back the stammer that was threatening to affect his voice and pointed a shaking finger towards it.

"Oh, I'm glad you noticed dad."

"I had to wait ages for that, they're my own initials, KEH 1, Kerry Edwin Heatherington the first.

The judge nodded his head, the thoughts of his last case of the day and the name, Karen Elizabeth Holt raced into his mind.

"It came from a wrecked Jaguar in the local scrap yard, I'm dying to get onto the motorway with It."

OTHER BOOKS BY ELISA WILKINSON

TRUE GHOST STORIES

1/RESTLESS SPIRITS is in book form and audio (New Generation publisher)
2/ SEEING IS BELIEVING (Austin MacAuly) publisher

FICTION

1/ DARK OAKS
2/ GATEWAY TO HELL
3/ THE LAKE
These three books are a trilogy and follow on from one another.
4/ THE HAUNTING OF CHURCH COTTAGE
5/ THE HAUNTED ASYLUM
Five books published by New Generation publishers
6/ GOLDBURGH HALL (Austin Macauly publishers)

TRUE WAR STORIES & PHOTOS

Before and throughout WW1 & WW2 to The peacetime of the present day. (Austin Macauly publishers)

BACK PAGE COVER.

Elisa lives at Thornes, Wakefield with her husband Eric. Both are now retired, Eric however works from home with other interests, and Elisa is still writing books.

As a young child Elisa was raised by her grandparents, Edith and Robert Clayton, at Lake Lock Road, Stanley, West Yorkshire. She regularly attended St Peters church and was educated at St Peters and Stanley modern schools.

She has lived in South Dakota USA, for over twelve years where she made many friends, her closest friends were Del Iron cloud who is a well-known artist, and Sonja Holy Eagle, who owns The Drum Company, in Rapid City, with whom she has shared many fresh doughnuts.

Elisa is a well-known and respected author her books include Seeing is Believing and Restless Spirits, all are true hauntings.

She has also written a book of war stories that include Photographs that were given to her by family members.

Her books Dark Oaks Gateway to Hell and The Lake are a trilogy, and are fiction.

Elisa does however, investigate all kinds of phenomena with her daughter Lesley Anne. These include, UFO, Hauntings, and Poltergeist activity.

Elisa follows the Pagan faith and she respects all forms of nature and wildlife, she also has a strong conviction that our planet earth is a living essence.

Milton Keynes UK
Ingram Content Group UK Ltd.
UKHW032226021124
450552UK00001B/4